HUXLEY and FlaPjack

RACE TO THE RESCUE

Wibbleton

Dingle Island

JollyGoods

More Shops

N
W   E
S

To the fabulous Hough family –
bigguns and littluns
– AM

To my very young friends Mic, Issu and Raphael.
Our big adventure is all your fault! xxx – FG

LITTLE TIGER
An imprint of Little Tiger Press Limited
1 Coda Studios, 189 Munster Road, London SW6 6AW

Imported into the EEA by Penguin Random House Ireland,
Morrison Chambers, 32 Nassau Street, Dublin D02 YH68

First published in Great Britain in 2023

Text copyright © Alan MacDonald, 2023
Illustrations © Francesca Gambatesa, 2023

ISBN: 978-1-78895-417-4

Printed and bound in China.

STP/3800/0499/0323

MIX
Paper | Supporting
responsible forestry
FSC® C144853

The Forest Stewardship Council® (FSC®) is a global, not-for-profit organization
dedicated to the promotion of responsible forest management worldwide. FSC defines
standards based on agreed principles for responsible forest stewardship that
are supported by environmental, social, and economic stakeholders.
To learn more, visit www.fsc.org

2 4 6 8 10 9 7 5 3 1

HuxLEY and FlaPjack

RACE TO THE RESCUE

ALAN MACDONALD   **FRANCESCA GAMBATESA**

LiTTLE TiGER
LONDON

Some koala bears are shy, timid creatures.

Huxley *isn't* that sort of bear.

He lives with his best friend Flapjack
in a rambling tree house by the woods.
Huxley's bedroom is high in the treetops
where he sleeps in a hammock with
a view of the stars.

Flapjack is a small, rather worried
penguin. His bedroom is on the ground
floor because he's scared of heights.

For Huxley and Flapjack, every day
is a new adventure...

Chapter One

One morning Huxley awoke to a delicious smell.

"Pancakes! Yum! My favourite!" he said, tumbling out of his hammock.

He slid down a rope ladder to the kitchen where Flapjack was juggling a pancake in a frying pan.

"Morning, Flapjack! They smell good!" said Huxley, throwing himself into a chair.

"This one's almost ready if it doesn't escape," said Flapjack.

He flipped the pancake high into the air.

Huxley shot out his plate just in time to catch it.

"Mmm, scrummy!" he said, wolfing it down in one bite. "Now what shall we do today?"

Ding-a-ling! A bell tinkled below.

"Post for you, Huxley!" cried the postwoman.

Huxley bounded to the window
and pulled up a basket.

"Thank you, Zoe!" he called.

Inside were a few letters and parcels.

"Oh, look, a postcard from Aunt Lolly in America," said Huxley. "I think this one is a book for you, Flapjack, and hooray – a new set of paints for me! But what's this?"

GRAND OPENING

Jolly Goods

The shop that sells everything. Don't miss it!

Today!

"Woo-hoo! That's what we'll do today —
go to the grand opening in town!" cried
Huxley excitedly.

Flapjack looked worried. "Are you sure,
Huxley? Last time we went to town you
fell in the fountain, remember?"

"Oh yes, so I did," chuckled Huxley.
"I won't be making that mistake again!
Eat up, Flapjack, I've got my pocket
money to spend."

Huxley rushed to get dressed while Flapjack
fetched his bobble hat in case it rained
or snowed – or both. Then they set off,
wobbling down the path on their tandem.

Flapjack did the pedalling while Huxley
was in charge of steering and shouting
directions.

"Turn right!"

"This way!"

"Mind that herd of cows!"

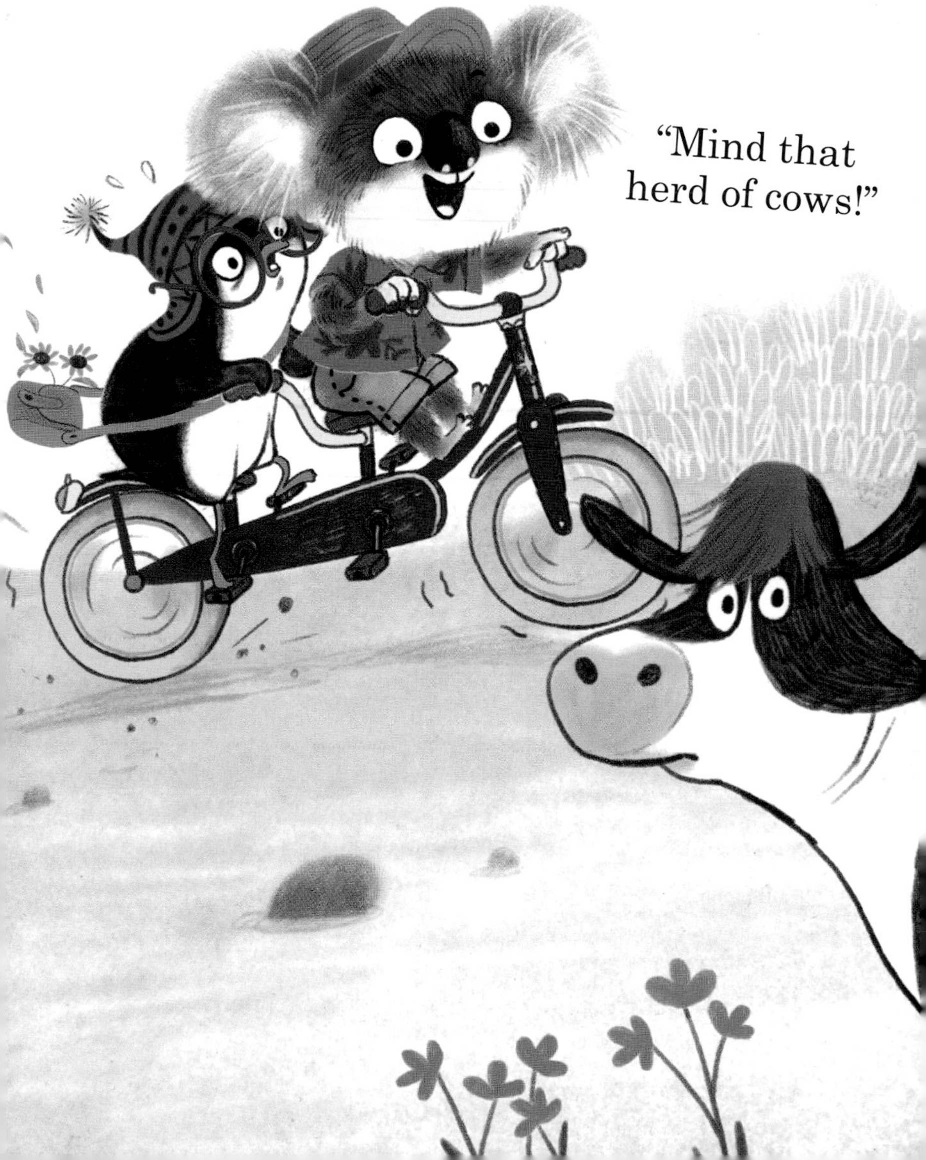

After a long, bumpy ride they arrived
in town.

The square was bustling with people.
Huxley greeted their friends at the
shops and the school.

"Hello, Bella, save us some cakes!"

"Good morning, Miss Flute!
Hello, children!"

Over the humpback bridge, Huxley waved to Sammy setting tables at his café.

Then on they whizzed down the high
street. Suddenly Huxley braked so hard
that Flapjack almost flew out of his seat.

"Why have we stopped?" he asked.

"There it is … JollyGoods!" cried Huxley.
"Holey underpants! It's huge!"

JollyGoods was the biggest shop they'd
ever seen. It had more windows than
you could count and a grand
entrance hung with flags.

Flapjack parked the tandem outside. Then
they hurried in through the revolving doors
– and came back out on to the street again.

"This door doesn't work," said
Huxley, puzzled.

"Maybe it's like a merry-go-round and you
have to wait till it stops?" said Flapjack.

They went round and round until finally
they stumbled inside. Flapjack felt so
dizzy he had to lie down on a pile of fluffy
towels.

The store manager came marching over.

"Ahem. Can I help
you, sir?" he asked
stiffly.

Flapjack sat up.

"Um, no thanks, I'm feeling better now," he said, and hurried off to find Huxley.

The store was crowded with shoppers. Huxley did a little dance of excitement. There were so many floors he hardly knew where to start.

He tried asking a woman, who was standing near the escalators.

"Excuse me, which floor is the hat department?"

But the woman didn't answer or even look round.

"Well, really! How rude!" said Huxley.

Flapjack tugged at his arm.

"Huxley, she can't hear you, she's a shop
dummy!" he explained.

They checked the store guide and took the escalator.

On the first floor they found hats in every style.

Huxley tried on a top hat and an artist's black beret. He looked dashing in a Russian fur hat and handsome in a deerstalker.

Flapjack tried on a sombrero but it was a little too big for him.

The store manager hovered nearby, keeping an eye on them.

On the second floor they found the sports department.

"I bet I'd be good at tennis," said Huxley, swishing a racket.

He switched on a machine, which began firing tennis balls.

WHIZZ!

WHOOSH!

THUNK!

"Wahoo!" cried Huxley, swiping and missing with his racket.

Flapjack hurriedly turned the machine off.

"Let's try something less dangerous," he suggested. "How about tiddlywinks?"

But Huxley had seen something much
more exciting.

"Look! A trampoline!" he gasped.

In no time he'd clambered on and was
bouncing up to the ceiling.

"Whee! Look at me!"

"Do be careful,"
warned Flapjack.

But Huxley kept bouncing ... higher and higher until he flew right off and landed in someone's arms.

"You again!" groaned the store manager.

"That is the bounciest trampoline ever," Huxley told him. "You should try it!"

Chapter Two

JollyGoods was amazing. Huxley insisted they visit all six floors because he loved riding the escalators.

He ran up all the 'Up' escalators...

Then down all the 'Down' ones. Flapjack got out of breath trying to keep up.

Then, just as they were heading up to the toy department...

...someone shot past on a skateboard.

"Yikes! Who was that?" asked Huxley.

"I've no idea but he should slow down before he causes an accident," said Flapjack.

On the fourth floor the store manager was waiting for them. Huxley hurried past, picking up one toy after another.

"Huxley, you can't buy *everything*. You have to make up your mind," pleaded Flapjack.

Huxley wasn't good at making up his mind. Luckily something had just caught his eye...

The perfect outfit for a daring bear who loved adventures!

SUPER GUY

Huxley wasted no time in trying it on.

"How do I look?" he asked.

"Oh, very smart, like a superhero," said Flapjack.

"I *am* a superhero," said Huxley.

"Faster than a speeding squirrel,
Stronger than a stinky cheese,
It's Super Huxley to the rescue!"

Super Huxley could lift heavy trucks above his head.

He could leap over tall buildings.

And save the world with one hand!

The store manager tapped him on the shoulder.

"Excuse me, sir, I'll have to ask you to leave before you break something," he sniffed. "Are you buying that outfit?"

"You bet your boots I'm buying it!" said
Huxley. "And don't bother to wrap it,
I'll keep it on."

They headed down to the
ground floor. Huxley waved
to all the shoppers staring at
his costume.

"So, Flapjack, what do you think my superpower should be?" he asked.

"Your *superpower?*" repeated Flapjack.

"Yes, maybe I could be invisible, or I've always wanted to fly."

"Huxley, *please*," sighed Flapjack. "You're a bear and bears can't fly."

But Huxley took no notice. He leaped off the escalator and ran towards the main door. Maybe if he got up speed he could take off?

ZOOOM!

Suddenly the skateboarder appeared again from nowhere and crashed straight into him.

They catapulted into the revolving doors
and tumbled out on to the pavement.

The skateboarder sat up, rubbing his head.

Jewels and watches had spilled from his
sack and he quickly pushed them back in.

Huxley stared at him in surprise.

"You're wearing my mask!" he said.

"Actually, *you're* wearing mine," said the skateboarder. "But I like your cape, mind if I take it?"

Before Huxley could answer it vanished into the sack.

"Well, nice bumping into you, sorry I can't stop," said the stranger. And jumping on to his skateboard, he zoomed off.

Flapjack came hurrying out of the shop.

"Huxley! Are you all right?" he asked anxiously.

"My cape! He took my cape!" moaned Huxley. "We have to go after him!"

"Is that a good idea?" asked Flapjack. "He's bigger than us. Maybe someone else ought to do it?"

Before Huxley could reply, an alarm began ringing and the store manager came running out.

"Stop! Thief!" he shouted.

"Oh my bedsocks! He means *you*, Huxley!" said Flapjack. "Come on, we better get out of here!"

They jumped on to their tandem and took off. Flapjack pedalled hard but Huxley wasn't taking them home.

"Where are we off to now?" asked Flapjack.

"To catch the skateboarder and get my cape back, of course," said Huxley.

"But Huxley, I think that skateboarder is a robber," panted Flapjack.

"Stop! Thief!" shouted a voice.

Huxley looked round to see the store manager chasing after them on a scooter.

Yikes! What next? he thought.

Chapter Three

Down the road they spotted the
skateboarder weaving along the pavement.

"Stop! Give me back my cape!" yelled Huxley.

"He won't stop, he just robbed JollyGoods," puffed Flapjack.

"Really? How can you be sure?" asked Huxley.

"Huxley, he was carrying *a big sack of jewels*!" said Flapjack.

"Oh yes, I thought that was odd," said Huxley. "But hang on, if he's a robber then why's the store manager chasing *me*?"

"Because you're both wearing the same mask!" said Flapjack. "The manager thinks *you're* the robber!"

Huxley shook his head. This sort of thing
shouldn't happen to a superhero.

They whizzed past traffic
and startled shoppers.

"Faster, Flapjack! We're catching him!" cried Huxley.

But the robber had seen them and he swerved into the park.

"Hold tight! Going left!" cried Huxley.

They raced down paths and bumped across the grass, scattering a flock of pigeons.

Finally they skidded to a halt.

"Holey underpants!" gasped Huxley. "Where did *they* all come from?"

Everywhere they looked skateboarders
were performing jumps, spins and flips.

But where was the masked robber?

"I think we lost him," sighed Flapjack.

But he spoke too soon...

Ha ha! Can't catch me!

"After him!" cried Huxley.

They doubled back through the park gates, almost knocking over the store manager on his scooter.

Huxley saw shops flash past.

They were heading back to the town square.

Outside Sammy's Café, people were having lunch.

The robber made straight for them. He zigzagged between the tables, swiping a sausage off a plate.

"Look out, Huxley!" cried Flapjack, shutting his eyes.

A table and dinner plates went flying.

"Help! It's all gone dark!" said Huxley.

He shook off the tablecloth, but more trouble lay ahead.

"Huxley, the bridge – brake... BRAKE!" yelled Flapjack.

But it was too late...

The skateboard rose high into the air ...
and landed safely in the square.

67

Next the tandem took off like a jet plane.

"Woo-hoo! We're flying!"
whooped Huxley.

"Oh no," gulped Flapjack...

Flapjack clambered out and wrung water
from his bobble hat.

Huxley sat down beside him.

"What did you say about not making the
same mistake again?" asked Flapjack.

"It's not my fault," said Huxley. "If you ask me, it's a silly place to put a fountain!"

The robber had escaped, but the chase wasn't quite finished.

A scooter came squeaking over the bridge.

The store manager jumped off, red-faced and out of breath.

"Right, you two, you're coming with me," he snapped. "You've got a lot of explaining to do."

Chapter Four

Back at JollyGoods, Huxley and Flapjack sat in the store manager's office, making puddles on the floor.

"Honestly, Mr Manager, it's all a big mistake," said Huxley. "We didn't steal any jewels or watches!"

"Then why were you running away?" the store manager demanded.

"Actually, we were cycling," Huxley pointed out.

"And we were chasing the *real* robber, the one on a skateboard," said Flapjack. "He's the one you need to catch."

"Humph. Well. Hmm," said the store manager.

He opened a drawer in his desk and took out a poster.

"This robber you saw, did he look like this?"

WANTED

FAST FINGERS FRANKIE

'The skateboard thief'

"That's him! The dirty rotten cape-pincher!"
cried Huxley.

"Never mind that," said the store manager.
"Fast Fingers Frankie has robbed a dozen
shops this year. The trouble is he's so quick
no one can catch him."

"I bet we could," said Huxley.

"Um, I don't know about that," said Flapjack.

"I do. Superheroes are good at that sort of thing," argued Huxley.

The store manager sat back. "All right, let's hear it, how *would* you catch him?"

"Well, um … obviously we'd need a clever plan, wouldn't we, Flapjack?" said Huxley.

But Flapjack wasn't listening. He was staring at a shop dummy stood in a corner of the office. Suddenly he jumped up.

"I've got it!" he cried. "We'll need posters, lots of them! And you can do one of your paintings, Huxley."

"You see!" said Huxley. "I told you we'd think of something."

That afternoon posters went up all over town.

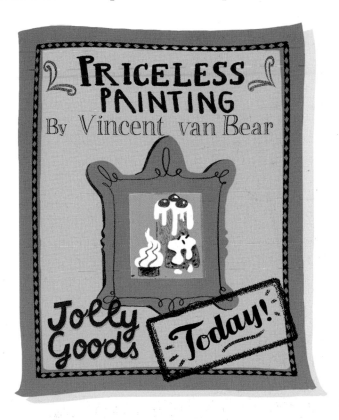

The 'priceless' painting turned out to be a splodgy picture of cream cakes.

It hung in JollyGoods' shop window in front of a curtain.

On either side of it stood a shop dummy.

One was dressed as an artist in a smart black beret.

The other wore a wig and posed as a model.

The artist was painting a portrait on his easel, but he was having trouble keeping still.

"Huxley!" hissed Flapjack.

"I can't help it, I've got an itchy nose," muttered Huxley. "How long do we have to stand like this?"

"Until Fast Fingers Frankie gets here," said Flapjack. "Try to be patient."

By five thirty the last customers were leaving the shop.

JollyGoods was closing up.

Huxley's arm ached from holding a paintbrush.

"He's not coming," he sighed. "We may as well give up."

Just then something flashed past the shop window.

ZOOOM!

"Yikes on a bike! Did you see that?" asked
Huxley.

"Shh! It's him," whispered Flapjack. "Don't
make a sound."

Before long the curtain twitched and a sly face peeped in. Fast Fingers Frankie slipped into the shop window with his sack.

He stared at the two shop dummies.

The one in the beret looked strangely familiar.

He poked the funny dummy in the tummy. Huxley tried not to move or giggle.

"Ha! Just a stupid pair of shop dummies!" said Fingers to himself.

He turned to the priceless painting and reached up to grab it…

"NOW!" squeaked Flapjack.

Huxley seized the portrait from his easel and brought it down over Fingers' head.

WHUMP!

"OWW! I've been framed!" moaned
Fingers.

Flapjack pulled off his wig.

"That'll teach you to take things that don't belong to you," he said, wagging his flipper.

"And that's my cape you're wearing," said Huxley. "I'll have it back, if you don't mind."

The store manager was delighted. In Fingers' sack they found all the watches and jewels he'd stolen that morning.

"He won't be robbing any more shops, thanks to you," said the manager. "On behalf of JollyGoods please accept this as a small reward."

Huxley put the money in his pocket.

"It was nothing really," he said. "I'm just glad that my clever plan worked out."

Flapjack blinked.
"*Your* clever plan, Huxley?"

"Goodness, is that the time?" said Huxley. "We really should be getting home for tea. And luckily I know just the place to spend our reward."

Back at the town square they rescued their tandem from the fountain and called in at Bella's shop.

"Hello, Bella! Did you save us some cakes?" asked Huxley.

"For you, Huxley, of course!" laughed Bella.

Back home, they sat down to a feast of
strawberry tarts, sticky doughnuts
and pink iced buns.

"Are you *ever* going to take that cape off?"
asked Flapjack.

"Certainly not!" said Huxley. "In fact I've
just discovered my superpower. I can make
things disappear!"

"Really? How?" asked Flapjack.

Huxley jumped up, grabbed an iced bun
and ate it in one go.

"You see!" he cried, with his mouth full.

"Super Huxley
strikes again!"

Huxley yawned. He was ready for bed.

Overhead the stars were
coming out in the sky.

Tomorrow was another day.

Who knew what adventures lay
in store for a daring bear?

Look out for more

HuxLEY and FlapJack

stories coming soon!